Crius and the
Night of Fright

HEROES IN TRAINING

TRAINING

Crius and the Night of Fright

Joan Holub and
Suzanne Williams

Aladdin

NEW YORK LONDON TORONTO SYDNEY NEW DELHI

For our heroic readers:

*Christine D-H and Kenzo S., J. Luman, Brenden S., Sven S., Xander
D., Calvin E. and Anthony D., Stephan R., the Andrade Family, Tait
L., Ariel S., Colin S., Caitlin R., Hannah R., Medolia S., Jakob W.,
Luke O. and Sophia O., Micah V., Taddy V., Kiki V., Pinki S., Jenny
C., Sara S., Joey W., John K., Lana W., and you!*

—J. H. and S. W.

If you purchased this book without a cover, you should be aware that this book is stolen property. It was reported as "unsold and destroyed" to the publisher, and neither the author nor the publisher has received any payment for this "stripped book."

This book is a work of fiction. Any references to historical events, real people, or real places are used fictitiously. Other names, characters, places, and events are products of the authors' imagination, and any resemblance to actual events or places or persons, living or dead, is entirely coincidental.

ALADDIN

An imprint of Simon & Schuster Children's Publishing Division
1230 Avenue of the Americas, New York, NY 10020
First Aladdin paperback edition April 2015
Text copyright © 2015 by Joan Holub and Suzanne Williams
Illustrations copyright © 2015 by Craig Phillips
Also available in an Aladdin hardcover edition.
All rights reserved, including the right of reproduction
in whole or in part in any form.
ALADDIN is a trademark of Simon & Schuster, Inc.,
and related logo is a registered trademark of Simon & Schuster, Inc.
For information about special discounts for bulk purchases,
please contact Simon & Schuster Special Sales
at 1-866-506-1949 or business@simonandschuster.com.
The Simon & Schuster Speakers Bureau can bring authors to your live event.
For more information or to book an event,
contact the Simon & Schuster Speakers Bureau at 1-866-248-3049
or visit our website at www.simonspeakers.com.
Cover designed by Karin Paprocki
Interior designed by Mike Rosamilia
The text of this book was set in Adobe Garamond Pro.
Manufactured in the United States of America 0315 OFF
2 4 6 8 10 9 7 5 3 1
Library of Congress Control Number 2015932178
ISBN 978-1-4814-3507-9 (hc)
ISBN 978-1-4814-3506-2 (pbk)
ISBN 978-1-4814-3508-6 (eBook)

⚡ Contents ⚡

Greetings, Mortal Readers,

I am Pythia, the Oracle of Delphi, in Greece. I have the power to see the future. Hear my prophecy:

Ahead, I see dancers lurking. Wait—make that *danger* lurking. (The future can be blurry, especially when my eyeglasses are foggy.)

Anyhoo, beware! Titan giants seek to rule all of Earth's domains—oceans, mountains, forests, and the depths of the Underwear. Oops—make that *Underworld*. Led by King Cronus, they are out to destroy us all!

Yet I foresee hope. A band of rightful rulers

called Olympians will arise. Though their size and youth are no match for the Titans, they will be giant in heart, mind, and spirit. They await their leader—a very special boy. One who is destined to become king of the gods and ruler of the heavens.

If he is brave enough.

And if he and his friends work together as one. And if they can learn to use their new amazing flowers—um, amazing *powers*—in time to save the world!

CHAPTER ONE
Zap!

"Come on, guys. Run for the hills!" Ten-year-old Zeus yelled to the eight Olympians around him.

He looked behind him. Some Cronies—half-giant soldiers in King Cronus's army—were charging toward the Olympians across the plains.

"Where are you tasty tidbits going, Snackboy?" one of the Cronies called out as they stomped toward Zeus and his friends.

Anger rose inside Zeus. It seemed like they couldn't go anywhere without the Cronies finding and threatening to gobble or clobber them.

Ares, the god of war, ran up next to him. His red eyes were blazing.

"There are only six of them, and nine of us!" he said. "We should stop and fight!"

"They're five times as big as we are, and ten times as strong!" Zeus reminded him. "Do the math."

"But we have powers!" Ares argued.

"It's too risky," Zeus said. "It's my job to keep everyone safe. I say we hide in the hills up ahead and figure out our next move."

Pythia, the Oracle of Delphi, had told Zeus that he was the leader of the Olympians. Ever since then, he felt responsible for their safety. Unfortunately, they were usually in danger, so the responsibility was a huge one!

For some reason, King Cronus—a Titan

almost as tall as the hills up ahead—and the other Titans wanted to do away with them. Zeus hadn't even known he was an Olympian until the Cronies had captured and taken him to Cronus a while back. Zeus smiled to himself, recalling how he'd rescued five Olympians— Hades, Poseidon, Hera, Demeter, and Hestia— by making the king barf them up from his belly!

Ever since then, Pythia kept appearing to them in a hazy mist to send them on quests. She gave them hints that were not too helpful (her foggy glasses sometimes meant things got lost in translation), but they always managed to figure them out just in the nick of time. And only a short time ago, she told Zeus that the Olympians Cronus had barfed up were his brothers and sisters!

They had also found three more Olympians on their journeys: Ares, Athena, and Apollo. Together, the nine Olympians had fought monsters, battled

Titans, and been chased by countless Cronies.

And this quest was no different. Pythia had sent them to find yet another Olympian—Apollo's sister, Artemis. Sure, it had been smooth sailing at first. They'd left from the new city of Athens, crossed the Gulf of Corinth, and landed safely. But then the Cronies had pounced.

Hearing a shriek, Zeus looked over his shoulder. It was a Crony shrieking in pain. He had made a grab for Hestia! Luckily, she had thought fast. She'd used her magical object—a torch that could create fire and send it anywhere—to lash back at him. Safe now, she was catching up to the Olympians again.

"I'll get you for that!" yelled the Crony. He and his half-giant buddy charged closer and closer. Their muscled chests were bare. Some of them had tattoos or beards. Each carried a shield and a weapon—either an enormous club or a sharp sword. Basically, they were scary-looking!

"If we can make it to the hills, we might lose them!" Zeus shouted toward the others.

The rocky hills ahead were filled with cracks, caves, and crevices: the perfect cover for small Olympians to hide from half-giant Cronies.

"Ha-ha! No way! You can't escape us, Olympians!" one of the Cronies growled. And then another sound filled the air.

"Yow!" It was Poseidon yelping in pain.

He had tripped over his trident—a three-pronged magical weapon that looked sort of like a pitchfork. Now he was sprawled facedown in the dirt.

Demeter quickly stopped and reached out a hand to help him up. Poseidon tried to stand. He winced and then fell right back down.

"I think I did something to my ankle," he said. "You guys need to keep going!"

Demeter paused, her eyes filled with concern.

"*Go!*" Poseidon yelled at her.

"No! Not without you!" Demeter cried.

The other Olympians hadn't even noticed that Poseidon was down. Zeus waved Demeter on and doubled back toward his brother.

Unfortunately, one of the Cronies got to Poseidon first. The half-giant grinned a cruel smile. He raised his club above his head.

"No! Leave him alone!" Zeus bellowed in a voice like booming thunder. A surge of panic flowed through him. There was no way he could get there in time! He grabbed the lightning-bolt-shaped dagger that hung from his belt. He had found Bolt, one of his magical objects, in the temple at Delphi where he'd first met the Oracle. It had been the beginning of his epic quest to gain power for the Olympians.

Once drawn, the dagger immediately sprang to its full size—five feet long—and gleamed in his hand. He raised his arm, holding it skyward as a terrible anger filled him. "Get the Crony!" Zeus yelled, hurling Bolt in the half-giant's direction.

Zap! Bolt shot forward and struck Poseidon's half-giant attacker. The Crony flew backward, slamming into the Crony behind him, who slammed into another behind *him*, knocking them down like dominoes.

At the same time, dark, angry storm clouds that mirrored Zeus's anger gathered in the sky above them. A storm wind whipped up out of nowhere. Lightning streaked down from the clouds, sending the Cronies scattering.

Meanwhile, Demeter and Hades returned to grab Poseidon. They each lifted him up by one arm and helped him limp away. They and the other Olympians stared at Zeus, wide-eyed. It seemed like he must be causing the storm. But he didn't notice. More anger filled him, darker

and blacker. The fury of the storm grew blacker too. Bolt had returned to Zeus and he held Bolt above him as the wind whipped around him.

"Has he always been this powerful?" asked gray-eyed Athena, who had only been with the group a short time.

"No, this is new, and a little worrisome, I have to admit," replied Hera, brushing her blond hair to the side as the two girls eyed Zeus in surprise. "Make sure everyone gets to the hills, okay? I'll go help him fight."

Zap! Zap! Zap! Zeus blasted the Cronies with Bolt one by one. The ones who weren't hit were running away like scared mice.

"Zeus!" Hera cried. Rain lashed at her face as she ran up and tried to get his attention.

But he didn't reply. It was like he was in a trance.

"Zeus!" she yelled louder. Still nothing. She shook him by the shoulders. "Come on! You've got to stop before your crazy storm zaps us too."

Zeus blinked suddenly as her words finally got through to him. What was he doing? This storm of his was getting out of control! "Bolt! Small!" he cried.

Zzpt! His thunderbolt shrank to dagger size, and he rammed it under his belt. Then he and Hera took off running. They quickly reached the hills.

They found the other seven Olympians huddled there together, getting drenched by the rain. Demeter was wrapping a piece of cloth around Poseidon's ankle. They all looked at Zeus in concern and wonder.

"Thanks for saving me out there, bro," Poseidon said. "But where did all that crazy storm power come from? That was awesome."

"I have no idea," Zeus said, which was true.

And that scared him plenty!

CHAPTER TWO
Wild Winds

e need to find shelter," Zeus said, quickly slipping back into leader mode.

"Too bad there aren't any caves on this side of the hill," said Hades. His black hair was matted to his forehead, wet from the downpour. As the ruler of the Underworld, he was drawn to dark, closed-in spaces. "Nothing big enough to hold us, anyway."

"Well, we can't stay out in this," Hera said.

She looked at Zeus. "You started this storm. Can't you stop it?"

He shook his head. "Usually they stop once I put Bolt away, but—"

"Let's get going. Maybe we'll find shelter on the other side of the hill," Athena interrupted hopefully. "Hestia, we might need your torch to light the way."

Hestia frowned. "I'm not sure if my magic flame can stand up to this wind and rain. But I can try it."

Apollo held out his hand, palm up. "I think the rain is slowing down. Now is a good time to get out of town."

"We're not in a town," Hera pointed out.

Apollo shrugged, grinning. "I know. But it rhymes!" said the musical Olympian.

"Athena's right. Let's go," urged Zeus, and they made their way down a muddy path and around the hill. Poseidon's ankle still hurt him, so Hades and Demeter helped him.

They didn't find any caves on the other side. A small field stood between them and the next hill.

"Onward!" Zeus commanded, and as he spoke, the wind became stronger. The rain started to fall harder again too.

Hestia's torch flickered dimly as she led the way across the field. The wind howled around them.

"You could at least try to stop this storm. I mean, you did start it, right?" Hera asked Zeus in a grumpy tone.

"I'm not sure I started all this," Zeus said. "If I did, I didn't mean to. But I can't stop it," Zeus informed her.

Whoosh! The wind blew stronger. So strong that it knocked Hestia off her feet!

"I'm okay," she said, jumping back.

"Can your feather scout ahead and see if there's a cave?" Zeus asked Hera.

Hera protectively touched the bag that she

carried around her shoulder. She kept her magical object, a peacock feather, inside.

"I'm not taking the feather out in this mess," she said. "It might blow away and never come back!"

"Then use Chip!" Zeus urged.

Chip was another one of Zeus's magical objects, but he let Hera use it. She wore the stone on a leather string around her neck. Sometimes arrows would appear on Chip like a map, showing them all where to go. This had helped them get out of a lot of sticky situations!

Hera fished the amulet on the leather cord from her collar. She looked at Chip, tapped on it, shook it. "It's not working!" she announced.

"Wait! There's something up ahead!" Hestia cried out in excitement.

Her flickering flame lit up a tiny makeshift shepherd's hut sitting in the muddy field. It looked like it was made of straw and branches.

Zeus frowned. "It doesn't look too sturdy."

"I can't walk much longer," Poseidon said from behind him. "Maybe we should stop anyway."

Demeter and Hades helped Poseidon inside the hut. Athena and Ares slipped in after them.

"Oomph! Your lyre is poking me. There's no more room!" Ares said as Apollo tried to enter.

Zeus peered over Apollo's shoulder into the hut. Ares was right.

"Hey! Chip's working again," Hera yelled over the wind. "Let's move on. The rest of you can catch up to us in the hills when the storm stops!"

Ares nodded looked uncertain. "Should I go or stay? I'm the only one fierce enough to protect everyone but I can't be in two places at one time."

Zeus rolled his eyes. Sometimes Olympians were really full of themselves! "I don't like to split up, but I don't see any other choice. Find us when you can." With that, he, Hera, Apollo, and

Hestia continued on. The wind howled around them like a wild animal.

Plodding against the wall of wind, the four Olympians followed Chip's directions. The stone's glowing arrow led them to the safety of a cave. By then, they were drenched and shivering.

Hestia shook rain off her torch. "Campfire!" she said, pointing the torch at the ground. A cheerful orange fire immediately sprang up in the center of the cave. The Olympians huddled around it, trying to dry off.

Zeus looked back anxiously out at the field. "I hope the others will be okay in that hut."

"Ares said he'd look after them," said Hestia.

Hera snorted. "What's he going to do? Jab at the rain with his spear?"

"He means well," said Hestia kindly. "Besides, the others all have powers too. They'll be fine."

"Oh, really? Let's see," Hera said, warming her

hands over the fire. "Poseidon's trident can make water spring up anywhere. But I don't really think that'll help them right now, do you?"

"Hades has his invisibility helmet," Zeus reminded her.

"And what good is turning invisible in a storm?" Hera pointed out.

"Demeter's magic seeds could be what they needs, uh, need," Apollo sing-songed.

"Sure, she could magically grow food for them, but she always wants to save her seeds to help poor people. And Athena's aegis can turn things to stone, but if all this rain turned to stone we'd be in even more trouble."

"Don't forget she has a magic thread too," Hestia reminded her.

Hera nodded. "Right. That might be useful. But we haven't really seen what all it can do."

"I am the only Olympian without a magical

object," Apollo complained to Hera in a huffy voice. "Do you think I'm useless?"

Hera sighed. "Of course not. None of our magical objects can help stop this terrible storm. There's nothing we can do about it anyway." She looked at Zeus accusingly.

"It's not my fault," he protested, but deep down, he wasn't sure. He had felt some crazy kind of power inside him back there when Poseidon was in trouble. It hadn't seemed to come from Bolt, so where had it come from? Apollo took his lyre out of his bag. Even though it wasn't a magical object, he could make beautiful music with it.

Apollo strummed and began to sing.

> *"I hope this storm doesn't turn into*
> *a twister,*
> *So we can keep searching for my*
> *lost twin sister."*

Pythia had told them they would find Apollo's sister, if they could find a Titan called Crius. Apparently, the twins had been captured by another Titan, Iapetos, when they were three years old. They had escaped, but then lost track of each other.

Hestia put a hand on Apollo's arm. "We'll find her, Apollo. We've found every other Olympian that Pythia has sent us questing after."

Apollo nodded. "I hope you're right."

Suddenly, they heard a loud groaning sound outside. Zeus jumped up and ran to the mouth of the cave to look for the source of the sound.

Zap! Lightning flashed, illuminating the field. In that split second, Zeus saw the wind pick up the shepherd's hut. The hut whirled and swirled in the air—and then the wind carried it away!

"Noooooooo!" he wailed.

CHAPTER THREE

Into the Woods

Hera, Hestia, and Apollo ran up beside
Zeus. Their mouths opened in horror as
the wind carried the hut right over their
heads, and out of sight.

"We've got to go after them!" Zeus cried. "I'm
not losing any more Olympians!"

It seemed like on every one of their quests, the
Olympians had become separated. Zeus had sworn
to himself that he wouldn't let that happen again.
And now, five Olympians were flying away!

He bolted from the mouth of the cave, but Hera caught hold of his arm and pulled him back.

"No!" she said. "You'll only get blown away too. We have to wait until the storm dies down."

Hestia looked worried. "But that wind was so strong! What's going to happen when they crash down?"

Apollo strummed his lyre. "It'll splinter into wood. Which can't do anyone any good."

"Stop that!" Hera scolded. "This is not funny!"

"Sorry," said Apollo. "I'm freaking out too. But music calms me down."

"Music can be calming," Hera agreed. "But not with those lyrics!"

Hera, Hestia, and Apollo moved back around the fire. Frustrated, Zeus stayed by the cave entrance for a few minutes, staring at the storm. When he began shivering, he joined them around the magic flames. "It's not helping us to worry about the others when we can't do anything to help them right now.

Somebody introduce a new topic," he suggested.

"Okay. So, what do you think Crius will be like when we finally find him?" Hestia wondered. "Each Titan we've met has a different, scary power."

"Like Hyperion and his fireballs," Hera remembered.

"And Iapetus's power to freeze time," added Apollo.

Hestia shuddered. "I guess we won't know until we meet this creepy Crius face-to-face."

"Or better yet, sneak up on him," Zeus said. "Before he can show us his powers."

Hera yawned. "This storm is not going to end soon, I bet. We need to sleep, but I'm not sure I can."

Hestia looked at Apollo. "Got any songs that are calming enough to put us to sleep?"

Apollo nodded. Staring into the darkness outside the cave, he strummed his lyre again.

"Rain, rain, go away.

Come again some other day. . . ."

"It's catchy," Hera said, curling up on the floor

of the cave. "Not sure if it's a lullaby, though."

"I think lullabies will come easier when I finally look into my sister's eyes," Apollo replied. Then he began to play a sad, slow tune that soon had the girls yawning.

Zeus found himself yawning too and it didn't take long before he drifted off to sleep. Unfortunately, it wasn't a peaceful sleep. In his dreams, or rather his nightmares, he still saw the straw hut whirling and twirling in the wind.

They woke up to the sound of birds chirping. The first rays of morning sun streamed into the cave and across Zeus's face.

Apollo was already up, stretching, along with the rest of the group. "The storm is done! Here comes the sun!" he sing-songed happily. "Now we can go find Artemis."

"And that hut full of Olympians, don't forget," Hera reminded him.

"We should eat something first," Hestia suggested. "If we run into any monsters, we'll need our strength."

"Well, now that you've said that, I'm sure we *will* meet some monsters," Hera complained.

Zeus was anxious to get going, but his stomach felt like a hollow pit. "Breakfast is a good idea, thanks," he said.

Hestia looked in her bag. "Uh-oh. Our rations got wet. They're ruined!"

"Hold that dismal thought," Apollo said. He darted from the cave. Before anyone could ask what he was up to, he bounded back again with his arms full of ripe fruit. "Don't despair, just eat a pear. Some fell from a tree. Enough for you three and me!" Zeus knew he must be feeling hopeful again. He talked in rhyme most of the time—but especially when he was in a good mood.

Munching breakfast, they headed out again.

"We should find the others first," said Zeus. "That hut flew over the hill."

Hera held Chip in her palm. "Chip, where are the other Olympians?" she asked. A new arrow appeared on Chip's stone surface.

"This way," Hera said, pointing.

They followed the arrow and found a path that led to a thick forest. The morning sun was bright, but with tall trees blocking the sun, the forest looked dark and a little spooky.

"Think they landed in there?" Hestia said hopefully. "I hope falling through the trees didn't wreck their hut!"

"I'm sure they're fine," Zeus said quickly, though he wasn't sure of that at all. He was just trying to keep everyone's spirits up.

The sound of chirping birds faded as soon as the four Olympians entered the forest. It was eerily quiet as they wound their way through the trees.

"There's no sign of the others," Hera said.

"It's a big forest," Zeus said. "They'll turn up," he added, with less confidence than he felt. Then, out of nowhere, he shivered.

"What was that for?" Hera asked him.

"No clue," he replied. "I just suddenly felt . . . cold."

"I did too," Hestia said. "I've had that feeling before. It's usually right before monsters attack."

"Stop saying monsters!" Hera cried.

"Well, that's just what happens," Hestia pointed out.

"I know what she means," Zeus said. "It's not just a cold feeling. It's like my skin prickles. Right before something is about to happen."

Suddenly, Apollo cried out. "Look!"

Three spooky-looking girls had appeared on the path in front of them. They had pale green skin, dark green hair, and wild green eyes. Zeus couldn't tell if they were friends—or foes.

"What are you doing in our forest?" one of them demanded to know.

CHAPTER FOUR

The Dark Tower

Zeus stepped forward, forcing a smile. "We're looking for our lost friends," he said. "Five of them."

"And for my lost twin sister," added Apollo.

"And for a Titan named Crius," Hera said.

The green girls looked at one another.

"We can help you," said the one in the middle.

Zeus sighed with relief. "So, you don't want to attack us or anything?"

"We're tree nymphs," said the one on the right. "We don't attack—unless you're going to cut down our trees." She glared at them. "You're not here to cut down our trees, are you?"

"No!" Zeus said quickly. "Of course not."

The center one nodded. "Good. I am Carya, and these are my sisters, Orea and Telea."

"Nice to meet you," Zeus said. "He introduced himself and the other Olympians. So you said you can help us? Have you seen our five friends?"

Carya shook her head. "No. But we know where you can find Crius."

Orea looked at Apollo. "You! Golden-haired one. We've seen a girl who looks like you. Is your sister named Artemis?"

Apollo's eyes lit up. "Yes! Do you know where she is?"

Orea nodded. "Crius has her. He is using a potion of crushed flowers to keep her in a deep sleep."

"That's awful!" said Hera. "Why would he do that?"

"So she won't cause trouble. She was always trying to fight the Titans," replied Telea. "She is a good fighter."

Apollo smiled. "That's my sister."

"You said she's in a deep sleep," Zeus said. "Is there any way to wake her?"

Carya took a small pouch that hung around her neck and pulled a seed from it. This she handed to Hera, the nearest Olympian.

"Once planted, this seed will grow into a bush. Its berries can be used as a cure," Carya told them. "It is our gift to you all to help Artemis."

Apollo's smile faded. "But that will take so long!"

"If Demeter were here, she could make them grow fast," Hera pointed out.

"We'll find her. Hopefully in time to help," Zeus said firmly. "Thanks, Carya."

"You're welcome," Carya replied. Then she and the other two nymphs turned to leave.

"Wait! Where is Crius? Where is he keeping Artemis?" Apollo asked impatiently.

"Pass through our forest, and then head westward. You will soon see Crius's dark tower," Orea replied, turning back.

"But beware of the Pandi!" warned Telea.

"The Pandi? What are the Pandi?" Zeus asked.

"We must go," said Telea. With that, the nymphs seemed to dissolve right back into the trees.

"Wait! Come back! What are the Pandi?" Zeus yelled again, but the spooky nymphs did not reappear.

"Come on. Let's get to Crius's tower," Apollo said. His face looked fierce and determined—more like Ares than the Apollo that Zeus knew.

"We'll rescue Artemis, don't worry," Zeus promised him.

Apollo didn't say anything. He just stalked to the head of the group and marched them through the forest as fast as he could. The others almost had to jog to keep up with him.

In no time, they were out of the forest. A plain stretched out before them now, but there was no tower in sight.

"The nymphs said it wasn't far," Hestia said helpfully.

After walking another thirty minutes Apollo suddenly called a halt. "Look! The tower!"

He was right. It was impossible to miss on the horizon—and not just because it was tall.

Orea had called it a dark tower, Zeus remembered, but it wasn't just the tower that was dark. Though the sun was shining, the area surrounding the tower itself had no light. Bright stars shone above it. The group stared at the tower in awe.

"Now that is an incredible sight. We are in

day, but the tower's in night," rhymed Apollo.

"Must be some weird power Crius has," Zeus guessed.

As they got closer to the tower, they slowed their steps. The sky above them became darker and blacker as they approached it.

"On, flame!" Hestia commanded. A fire danced on one end of her torch. Zeus took Bolt from his belt and held it in front of him. Bolt glowed, trying to help.

The magical objects lit the way for a while. But the darkness became deeper and deeper.

"It's like the night is a thick woolly blanket," Hera remarked. "I can actually feel its darkness."

Whoosh! Something whizzed by Zeus's ear. Zeus caught a glimpse as it sped past him. An arrow!

"We're under attack!" he yelled.

"How can you tell?" Hera asked, spinning around. "I can't see anything!"

"Flame!" Hestia cried, and her torch burned brighter. She gasped.

The Olympians could now see their attackers clearly. A circle of strange big-eared warriors surrounded them. Each one had white hair covering his entire body. They gripped long spears with eight fingers on each hand, and they had eight toes on each foot to match.

"The Pandi, I'm guessing?" Apollo whispered to Zeus. "What big ears they have!"

"Hey! I heard that!" one of the Pandi yelled.

"Of course you did, with ears like that!" Hera laughed.

The Pandi poked her with the end of his spear.

"Ow!" Hera cried.

Then the Pandi grabbed the Olympians' weapons! They took Hestia's flame and Zeus's bolt. They even took Apollo's lyre, though it wasn't a weapon. "March!" Pandi ordered. One warrior got behind each Olympian, holding a sharp spear at the ready.

As they walked, the Olympians complained and asked annoying questions about where they were going in hope of distracting their captors. But their questions seemed to fall on deaf pointy ears.

Zeus's mind raced trying to think of a way to reclaim their weapons and escape. Then it came to him. Hera's feather! The Pandi hadn't taken it.

"Hera, command your feather to tickle them, so they'll drop their weapons," Zeus whispered to her. "Then we can run for it. I'll summon Bolt, and then zap them if they get too close."

"Good plan," Hera whispered back. "Except that these big-eared guys can hear you when you whisper, genius."

Sure enough, two Pandi rushed over to them right away. Zeus groaned. How could he have forgotten those huge ears of theirs?

"Stop!" one commanded. "Turn over the feather too."

Hera glared at Zeus as she took her feather out of her bag and gave it to the Pandi.

And the botched plan is all my fault! Now we'll never escape! Zeus thought.

CHAPTER FIVE

Crius

Then it hit Zeus—Duh! All he had to do was shout "Bolt!" and his magical object would fly back to him. He'd already opened his mouth to yell when Hera jabbed him in the side with her elbow.

"What?" he asked. She gave him a warning look, as if she knew exactly what he was intending to do.

Zeus knew that Hera wasn't going to risk

talking because the Pandi would hear. So what was her objection? What was wrong with his plan to call back Bolt?

He played it over in his head. As soon as he yelled Bolt, it would fly back into his hands. He could start zapping Pandi. Easy peasy.

He looked around at the Pandi surrounding them as they made their way toward the tower. He quickly counted five . . . ten . . . twenty . . . too many to count! He couldn't zap them all. That must be what Hera was thinking. That he should wait until the odds were better.

He knew that was smart, but waiting while spears were pointed at you wasn't an easy thing to do.

If Ares were here, he'd be stabbing at these attackers with his own spear! He had always thought that Ares was too hotheaded. But now Zeus thought maybe he understood Ares better. Because he was really itching to fight!

He looked back at Hestia and Apollo. Hestia looked worried. Apollo had that same determined look in his eyes that Zeus had noticed before. The one that meant he was thinking of his sister.

By now the darkness was as black as ink all around them. Some of the Pandi held torches they'd lit with Hestia's flame. They marched the Olympians up a stone walkway to the looming tower.

When they reached the entrance, two of their captors opened the enormous wooden doors. *Creak!* Once inside, they made the Olympians climb up a spiral staircase. It took them up, up, up to the top of the tower, and spilled them out into a large, round room.

A massive throne sat in the center of the room, and in the throne sat a humongous Titan.

Zeus thought he would never get used to how big these giants were. Even seated, this one towered over the Olympians like an oak tree.

The Titan wore a deep purple cloak that sparkled with what looked like swirling galaxies of real stars. A set of big ram horns grew from his giant head.

"Olympians," he greeted them in a booming voice. "Welcome to the tower of the Highest Titan! I am Crius."

"Wait, that sounds familiar," Hera said slowly. "Didn't one of the other Titans we've met before call himself that?"

Crius coughed. "You may be thinking of my older brother Hyperion. He calls himself the High Titan. But I am the Highest Titan!"

"If he's your older brother, shouldn't he rank higher than you?" Apollo asked.

Crius frowned. "Silence!" he boomed,

sounding annoyed. Then he turned to the Pandi. "Bring them." With that, he headed up yet another flight of stairs.

Zeus felt a spear in his back again, as the Pandi marched them up the stairs behind the Titan. Crius led them to an outdoor rooftop garden.

"It's beautiful," Hestia whispered.

Zeus agreed. Soft grass grew beneath their feet. A large fountain bubbled in the center of the garden, shimmering in the starlight. White moonflowers grew on vines that snaked up the sides of the walls. But why bring them here? Zeus wondered.

Crius walked to a table in front of the fountain. It was laden with fruit, delicious looking cakes, and a glass bowl filled with a pale-blue liquid.

The Titan looked at the Pandi and clapped

his hands. "Serve our guests!" he ordered. On command, two Pandi stepped up and began filling four glass cups with the blue drink.

Zeus looked around. Only a few of the Pandi had come with them upstairs. Now the odds were a little more in the Olympians' favor, he realized. The Pandi handed each of them a full cup.

"Drink, and enjoy the hospitality of the Highest Titan!" Crius said.

Zeus looked at the other Olympians. Hera mouthed the words "Don't drink." Hestia and Apollo nodded. They remembered what the nymphs had told them about Artemis: *He is using a potion of crushed flowers to keep her in a deep sleep.*

What if this was the same potion? If they drank, they might become captives of Crius too—forever!

"Come, come. Drink up!" Crius commanded when they hesitated. "You must be thirsty after your long journey to my tower."

Zeus knew he had to distract Crius somehow, so he stepped forward. "Why are you being so nice to us?" he asked. "You're a Titan. Most Titans attack when they see us. They want to take us to King Cronus."

Crius laughed. "But I am the Highest Titan, as I told you. I do not answer to Cronus."

"You don't?" Zeus asked, truly surprised to hear this.

"He is too concerned with puny humans and their stupid earth. I care not for them. I care only for the heavens!" As he spoke, the stars on his robe glimmered and shimmered.

Zeus cast a look back at his friends. Their cups were empty. He noticed a small damp spot on the grass at their feet where they had dumped the potion. He just hoped Crius hadn't noticed. Fortunately the Pandi were busily occupied at the table.

He motioned meaningfully to Hera. It was time to dump his cup too. She stepped forward.

"Your stars are very beautiful, oh Highest Titan," she told him in an admiring tone.

Crius looked up at the sky, and in that moment, Zeus dumped out the contents of his own glass.

"Yes, they are beautiful, and they shine only on me!" he boasted. Then he looked back at the Olympians. "I'm glad to see you have drunk your fill. How are you feeling?"

Zeus stretched his arms high and pretended to yawn. "Very sleepy, Highest Titan."

Hera, Hestia, and Apollo copied him. "Yes, very sleepy."

Crius smiled. "Good, good."

Zeus lay down on the grass and pretended to fall sleep. The others did the same.

"Excellent!" they heard Crius say. Then the self-proclaimed Highest Titan clapped his hands. "Pandi, take them to the Chamber of Sleep!"

It was hard for Zeus not to move or open his eyes when he felt the eight-fingered hairy hands of a Pandi pick him up.

"Foolish Olympians," Crius said with a chuckle. "You shall remain asleep until the Titans rule! With you in my power, that day won't be long in coming."

The Pandi warrior carried Zeus down the stairs, then walked straight for a while, maybe down a long hall. It was hard to say exactly since Zeus didn't dare open his eyes. Finally, the warrior stopped and Zeus heard the sound of a door opening. *Squeak!*

The Pandi dumped him on something soft—a bed, he guessed. He heard three more thuds as the other Olympians landed on the bed with him.

"Sweet dreams," one of the Pandi said, and the others laughed. Then the door closed, and everything got quiet.

Zeus slowly opened his eyes. Overhead, he saw a dark sky with twinkling constellations—but he knew he wasn't outside. This had to be some kind of magical room.

He sat up, waiting as his eyes readjusted to the darkness. The other four Olympians were getting their bearings too. Wait! Only *three* other Olympians had come here with him. So who was the fourth?

"Artemis!" Apollo cried out. Sure enough, sleeping there in the center of the bed was a girl with long golden hair. She was Apollo's twin!

CHAPTER SIX

Unexpected Help

Shhhh!" Zeus warned the others. "Who knows how close by those big-eared Pandi are?"

The four Olympians stayed quiet for a moment, staring at Artemis. When there were no sounds of the Pandi returning, the friends began to talk again.

Apollo crawled across the bed and shook his sister. "Artemis! Artemis! Wake up!"

The girl shifted a little bit, but she did not wake

up. She looked a lot like Apollo, thought Zeus. Their golden hair and their faces were almost identical!

Hera pulled out the tiny seed the nymphs had given her. "I wish this thing could make berries faster. We need a cure now."

"There must be some other way to wake your sister up," Hestia said to Apollo.

Apollo looked thoughtful. Then his face lit up with an idea. "My sister is sweet but has ticklish feet!" he said. "Hera, give your feather a shake. Maybe we can tickle her awake!"

Hera looked at Zeus. "Do you think it's safe to call my feather here? What if the Pandi notice?"

"It's so dark everywhere in this tower," Zeus reasoned. "So maybe they won't. It's worth a try. If the Pandi come, we can hide the feather and pretend to be asleep again."

"Sounds good," Hera said. She thought for a minute. Her feather would do anything she told it to, but she had to speak in rhyme for it to work.

"Feather, please fly away from those Pandi, and fly right into my own right . . . um . . . hand-y!" she said.

"Hand-y?" Apollo teased her. "You couldn't think of a better rhyme, maybe—"

But before he could go on, Hera's peacock feather scooted in under the door and came floating right up to the bed.

"Obviously, my rhyme was just fine," Hera said haughtily. She handed the feather to Apollo. "You'd better do this, I think."

Apollo nodded and started to tickle the bottoms of Artemis's bare feet with the feather.

She started to twitch right away. Then her right foot kicked Apollo in the arm.

"Ow!" he cried.

"Shh!" everyone shushed him.

Suddenly, Artemis propped herself up on her elbows. She opened her eyes, but just a little bit.

"Artemis?" Apollo whispered in a hopeful voice.

"Whaaaaat?" Her voice sounded groggy.

"Come on. Get her on her feet!" Zeus urged.

It took all four of them to drag Artemis out of bed. Apollo and Hera had to hold her up. She couldn't walk on her own, and she kept closing her eyes.

"What do we do now?" Hestia asked.

"Maybe I can help," said a new voice.

They all gasped as Hades appeared in front of them! His magical invisibility helmet was tucked under his arm.

"Hades! You're okay!" Zeus exclaimed, trying not to shout in his excitement. "What happened to the hut? And what about the others? Is everyone else all right?"

Hades nodded. "It was pretty scary when that wind picked up our hut. But we landed on top of a nice big haystack next to a farm. Nobody got hurt except for some bumps and bruises. That hut is history, though. Broken to boards."

"How did you find us here?" Hera asked.

"A farmer told us about Crius's tower," Hades replied. "Seems all the villagers around here know about it. This place looked pretty spooky, so I put on my helmet and went invisible before I went inside to scout it out. That's when I saw you all being carried into this room by those hairy warrior guys. It looked like you were asleep."

"Just faking it," Zeus explained. "Crius gave Artemis a sleeping potion to put her in a deep sleep. He tried to do the same with us."

"Artemis?" Hades asked, just now noticing the extra Olympian. "You found Apollo's sister? Woo-hoo!"

"Shhhhh!" Zeus warned. "Those hairy warriors have huge ears. They can hear—"

Bam! Too late. The door burst open, and four Pandi warriors ran inside.

"What's going on here?" one of them growled.

CHAPTER SEVEN

Battle of the Stars

olt!" Zeus yelled. His magical object instantly flew back from the clutches of whichever Pandi had had it. It zipped down the hall and right back into his hand. "Large!" Zeus added, and Bolt grew to five feet long.

Zap! Zap! Zap! Zap! He aimed Bolt at the Pandi, knocking them off their feet. One of them dropped Hestia's torch and another dropped Apollo's lyre. Both Olympians snatched up their belongings.

"Let's go!" Zeus urged.

The Olympians followed him out the door and down, down, down the winding staircase. Hades, Hera, and Apollo helped half-drag, half-carry Artemis.

They made it all the way down the stairs and outside before a line of torch-carrying Pandi came marching toward them across the grass.

"Can we beat them?" Hera whispered to Zeus.

"I'm not sure," he said. "But we have to try."

With a loud cry, he aimed Bolt toward the line of Pandi. Hestia whipped out of her torch.

"Charge!" cried the Pandi commander. The warriors surged forward.

And then each and every one of them tripped! They fell facedown. Some of their torches sputtered out.

"W-what just happened?" wondered Zeus. But then he heard Athena's voice.

"Got them!" she cried. "Now let's wrap them up!"

Athena rushed out from the left side of the Pandi, and Poseidon rushed out from the right side. Poseidon wasn't limping any more! They each looked like they were holding something. Zeus couldn't see it, but he knew what it was: Athena's superthin, superstrong, magical Thread of Dread. She and Poseidon had used it to trip and lasso the Pandi!

"It's good to see you guys," Zeus called, grinning when he also saw Demeter and Ares run up behind them. All nine Olympians were united again! They'd creamed some of the Pandi, but others were slowly getting to their feet.

Zeus held up Bolt. "Time for talk later. Come on. We have to hurry. Let's supercharge."

The Olympians huddled together. The ones with magical objects held them up, touching them together. Zeus's Bolt. Poseidon's trident.

Hera's feather. Hestia's torch. Hades's helmet. Ares's spear. Athena's thread.

Whoosh! A blast of energy flowed through the objects. Bolt glowed like the brightest lightning. The flame on Hestia's torch danced tall and high. It lit up the battlefield so the Olympians could see what they were facing.

"Let's do this!" Zeus cried.

The huddle broke apart, and they turned toward the Pandi as more waves of them came. The warriors angrily aimed their spears and raised their clubs at the Olympians.

Zap! Zeus blasted the spear right out of a Pandi's hand.

Poseidon pointed his trident at a line of advancing warriors. A powerful wave of water flowed out, knocking them backward.

"Yee-haaa!" Athena cried, twirling her Thread of Dread like a lasso. It wrapped around a Pandi warrior. She pulled it hard, bringing him down.

"Have a taste of the Spear of Fear!" Ares cried, hurling his spear at another Pandi. The warrior ducked just in time, and Ares ran after the spear.

Hades put his helmet back on. Invisible, he ran around the field, delivering surprise pinches and noogies to the Pandi and pulling the spears and clubs from their hands.

While most of the Olympians fought, Hera and Apollo protected Artemis. Hera gave the nymphs' seed to Demeter. "I need you to grow this into a bush with berries—fast!" she urged.

Zap! Zeus took down another Pandi. They had almost taken out the whole Pandi army by now. Soon they'd be able to get away—far, far away from this creepy tower. But he'd forgotten something. Or rather, someone.

Suddenly the ground beneath their feet shook, and Zeus looked behind him. Crius had emerged from the tower. The stars on his robe glittered brightly. His eyes flashed with anger.

"You shall not escape!" he boomed. "Surrender!"

Zeus aimed Bolt at him. "Never!"

A jagged streak of lightning hit the Titan square in the chest. He staggered backward, but he didn't fall. Recovering, he stomped toward Zeus, his eyes filled with fury.

"You dare to attack the Highest Titan?" he yelled.

Crius pulled a star from his robe. It was like a saw blade with sharp jagged edges. Before Zeus could react, Crius hurled the star at him sideways. Zeus dodged to the right, but the star caught on to the end of his tunic. He felt an amazing force pull him backward as the star pinned him to a tree!

Crius stomped toward him and whacked Bolt from his hands. "This is over, Olympian!"

CHAPTER EIGHT

A Voice in the Darkness

Crius lowered his massive head and got in Zeus's face. To Zeus, the Titan's eyes looked as big as plates and his nostrils were like hairy tunnels.

"Think you're special just because you're the son of the mighty Cronus?" Crius taunted. "You? A scrawny boy? I don't know why your daddy is so afraid of you. Without your little lightning bolt, you are nothing. Like a night with no stars."

"Soon your daddy's army will be here, and they will take you to him," Crius said. "And that will be the end of you. And all your little friends. For what chance will they have without their leader?"

A jolt of anger flowed through Zeus—like the one he'd felt battling the Cronies, only bigger. He yanked at his sleeve, freeing himself from the tree. Then he leaped onto Crius's robe, grabbing on to stars, reaching for him like they were rocks on a climbing wall to make his way down to the ground.

"Get back here, you little bug!" Crius fumed, reaching for him.

"Bolt!" Zeus yelled.

Pzzt! Bolt flew back to his hand lightning fast. The anger filling Zeus's heart flowed into the magical object, causing it to crackle and sparkle with energy. He heard his Olympian friends calling to him, but their voices seemed far away. It was as if the force of his anger was keeping them back from this one-on-one battle.

"Perhaps you are like Cronus after all. You have his anger," Crius said and then he laughed. "Are you going to sting me again, little bee? What good will that do you?"

"Bolt, now!" Zeus thundered. At this command, a massive burst of energy exploded from Bolt.

Boom! This time the blast was so strong it knocked Crius right off his feet. The giant toppled backward, shaking the ground as he fell.

Zeus leaped up onto his chest. He plucked stars from Crius's robe as fast as he could. Then, one by one, he hurled them at the flaps of the Titan's robe, pinning down Crius with his own stars!

"How dare you!" Crius roared in outrage. "Free me at once!"

Zeus marched up to the Titan's chest and

stared into his face. "I'll think about it," Zeus said. "If you tell me how I can defeat Cronus!"

Crius laughed. "You? Defeat the mighty Cronus? Impossible!"

"I don't think so. I just pinned down the Highest Titan, didn't I?" Zeus said, folding his arms in satisfaction. "Cronus must have a weakness. Tell me what it is!"

"By my honor as a Titan, I will not!" Crius replied, struggling to free himself.

Around him, the other Olympians were winning the battle with the Pandi. But Zeus didn't even notice. He was filled with anger at this big, bloated Titan.

He thinks I'm puny? Zeus raged. *He thinks I'm powerless? I'll show him!*

Zeus jabbed Bolt into the center of Crius's forehead. Bolt sizzled and sparked. *"Tell me!"* he thundered. "Or else."

"Never!" replied Crius.

Zeus's hand trembled. Crius wasn't going to give in. One blow from Bolt, and there would be one less Titan to worry about.

You have his anger, Crius had said. Is that what was happening? Was he going to end up as evil as King Cronus?

"Zeus!"

It was a woman's voice. Rhea's voice. His mother. Instantly it snapped Zeus out of his rage. He jumped off Crius's chest.

"Rhea? Mom?" he cried, and then he ran into the darkness to look for her.

CHAPTER NINE

A New Magical Object

"Rhea?" Zeus was sure he had heard his mother's voice. So where was she? Bolt's light went dim, and he stared into only blackness.

"Zeus, I am here," Rhea's voice replied.

His heart leaped. He hadn't known his mom while growing up. A goat and a magic bee named Melissa had raised him. Learning that Rhea was his mom had been the best thing about becoming an Olympian. But he had never met her face to face.

"Do not shine Bolt's light on me," Rhea said. "I have been watching over you. But if Cronus or any of the Titans learn this or see us talking, I will no longer be able to do so."

"I understand," Zeus said, but he felt sad. He really wanted to see his mom's face!

"Zeus, I see the storm inside you," Rhea said gently. "I want to help you."

"Crius said that I am like my father," Zeus admitted. "But Cronus is evil. Am I evil? Do my powers make me evil?"

"Power is neither good nor evil," Rhea replied gently. "It is what you do with your power that matters. Everyone has it in them to do good things or bad things—but whether or not we are good or bad is all up to the choices we make."

Zeus thought about this. "But I felt so

angry just now . . . like I couldn't control it. It has happened before."

"I understand," Rhea said. "You are young, Zeus. It is difficult to take control of your emotions. But you can do it. I know you can, my son."

My son. Hearing the words made Zeus suddenly well up with tears.

"I can?" he asked softly.

"You may be your father's son, but you are my son also," Rhea said. "When I was young, I made some bad choices. But then I learned to make good ones. I know you will make good choices, Zeus. You and the other Olympians have made many good choices already. You are kind to one another and to the mortals you meet. You help those in need."

Zeus nodded. "Yeah, I guess we have done that."

"And I know you will continue to make good choices," Rhea said. "You will triumph over your

father when the time comes. I have faith in you."

Warmth filled Zeus, and a deep calm came over him. His mother had faith in him. His *mother*. "Thank you," he whispered.

"Zeus, is that you?"

He spun around. Hera and the other Olympians appeared behind him, lit up by Hestia's torch.

"It's Rhea! Our mom!" he cried, pointing.

Hestia aimed the torch into the darkness . . . but there was no one there. Rhea was gone.

"She was here!" Zeus insisted. "I just talked to her!"

"I believe you," Hestia said. "What did she say?"

"That she has faith in us," Zeus replied. "She says we will defeat Cronus when the time comes. And that we are making good choices."

"Well, I think a good choice would be to

escape from here before Crius gets free and those Pandi get back on their hairy feet," said Poseidon.

"Right!" Zeus said. "Hestia, lead the way."

Hestia marched forward, holding her torch high. As Zeus trailed her, he noticed that Artemis looked more awake now. She was leaning against Apollo, but mostly she was walking on her own—and still yawning.

"How did you wake her up?" Zeus asked.

"Demeter did her thing. And . . . presto! The nymphs' seed grew into a berry bush," Hera said.

"Unfortunately Poseidon was attacking one of the Pandi at the time, and his trident washed away most of the berries," Demeter added.

"Hey," Poseidon interrupted with a shrug. "It was in the heat of battle. Sorry."

"So anyway, I only had a few wake-up berries to give to Artemis. Which is why she's still yawning," Demeter finished.

Suddenly they stepped out of Crius's realm and into bright sunlight. It shocked the Olympians for a second—they had been living in darkness for hours.

"Wow, it's really fun to leave darkness for sun!" Apollo sing-songed, lifting his face to catch the rays.

"Don't worry. You didn't lose any of your tan," Hera teased him.

"So where to now?" Poseidon asked, looking around.

"Well, this is usually when Pythia shows up in a mist to tell us what to do next," Zeus said.

They all waited quietly for a moment, expecting the oracle to appear. But she didn't.

"That's weird," said Hera. "But if she won't come to us, maybe we should go to Delphi and find her," she suggested. "Back through the forest first though."

"Good plan," Zeus agreed. "And good work back there at the tower, everyone!" Proud smiles formed at his words as they made their way toward the forest of the nymphs.

Above them, the sun was just starting to sink into the sky. Darkness was falling, for real this time, not by magic. Apollo strummed his lyre and sang as they walked.

> *"My sister was in a deep, deep sleep.*
> *She was under the Titan's spell.*
> *But the Olympians came to her rescue,*
> *And Crius the Titan fell.*
> *Now she's awake and with me*
>   *once more,*
> *And I think that's really swell!"*

Artemis gave her brother a sleepy smile. "Thanks, brother," she said, yawning. "I've missed your songs. That was a good one."

Soon they reached the woods. They hadn't gone far when the three green-skinned nymphs appeared in front of them.

"Galloping green ghosts!" Poseidon cried out in alarm.

"Calm down, Poseidon," Hera said. "They're tree nymphs. Friendly ones."

Carya stepped forward, her face delighted. "Artemis? Is that you?"

Artemis's blue eyes widened. "Carya?" she asked with a yawn.

"How do you know these nymphs?" Apollo asked his sister.

Carya answered for her. "She rescued us once. She was being taken to Crius's tower when she saw a river god about to swallow us up. She broke free from the Pandi and pulled us to safety. But then the Pandi captured her again, and we couldn't help her."

"You did help her though," said Demeter, stepping forward. "I mean, your berries did. They woke her up, but not all the way. Do you have any more of those magic seeds?"

Orea shook her head. "I am sorry. We gave Hera the only seed we had."

"But we do have something else for Artemis. A thank-you gift," said Telea. She held out her arms, and a long pouch with straps appeared in them. The feathery tops of arrows stuck out from the top of the pouch.

"A quiver with arrows," said Zeus. "Cool."

"We wove the quiver from the reeds," said Carya as Telea gave the gift to Artemis. "And the arrows are made from plants in our forest."

"Thank you," said Artemis with a yawn. Then she dropped to the ground. Using the quiver under her head as a pillow, she curled up to sleep.

"Oh dear," said Carya. "I see why you need more of those berries."

Apollo pulled Artemis to her feet. "Rise and shine, sleepyhead. Now is not the time for bed!"

Artemis opened her eyes again and yawned. Apollo hung the quiver around her shoulder for her.

"Thank you for all your help," Zeus told the green girls. "We won't forget you."

"And we won't forget you," the three nymphs said at the same time. Then they disappeared.

The Olympians continued on through the forest. When they emerged on the other side, the sun was low in the sky. Beautiful red and orange streaks spread across the horizon.

"We should find someplace to sleep for the night," said Athena.

"I'm sure Artemis would like that," Poseidon joked.

"I'll find a safe place," Hera said, placing the feather on her palm. "Feather, go see if there are Cronies we must fight, or if it's okay to go to sleep for the night!"

"Your rhymes are getting better," Apollo remarked as the feather floated away. They exchanged smiles.

Suddenly, a hazy mist materialized before them. A dark-haired woman appeared in it. She took off her glasses and wiped them off on her long white robe.

"Pythia!" Zeus cried.

CHAPTER TEN

Silver and Gold

Pythia put her glasses back on and sent Zeus and the others a fond smile.

"Welcome, Artemis!" she cried. "Now there are ten of you. How wonderful."

Artemis yawned.

"Oh dear," said Pythia. "Are you tired?"

"Crius gave her a potion that put her in a deep sleep," Zeus explained. "She took some berries as a cure, but we think she needs more."

Pythia squinted through her glasses. "My vision is hazy, but I believe she will be fully awake soon," she said. "I see she has a quiver. But she will need some magical silver arrows to fill it. And a gold bow so she can shoot those arrows."

"How is she supposed to get those?" Hera asked.

"You will find them on your next quest," Pythia replied. "Along with all the ammunition and armor you will need when you face Cronus and his Cronies."

"Does that mean we will finally battle Cronus himself on our next quest?" Zeus asked.

Pythia shook her head. "No. Not yet. You must find more Olympians first."

"More? How many are left?" Zeus asked.

"My spectacles are foggy. I am not sure," said Pythia, wiping off her glasses again. "But if you travel to the Island of Lemnos in the Aegean Sea, you will find another of your number."

"Can you tell us about the monsters we're sure to face?" Hera asked.

"Still too foggy," Pythia replied. "You should be on the lookout for silver lines and gold dolls!"

"Silver lines and gold dolls?" Zeus repeated. "That can't be r—" But before he could question Pythia further, the mist faded before everyone's eyes.

Hades laughed. "Ooh! Beware the gold dolls!" he said in a spooky voice.

Athena wiggled her fingers, trying to look scary. "And beware the silver lines!" Everyone laughed.

Zeus frowned. "That's funny, but I actually do wish we knew what we were going to be up against," he said. "What if it's some super terrible creature?"

"With long fangs," said Poseidon.

"And claws like knives," said Ares.

"And a spiked tail," added Athena.

"And a fire-breathing mouth!" said Hades.

"*Seven* fire-breathing mouths!" corrected Hestia.

Then they all cracked up.

"I hope you'll still be laughing when that monster really attacks," said Zeus.

Hera nudged him. "Oh come on, Zeus. When did you get so serious?"

Maybe when I realized that Cronus, our father, wants to destroy us, Zeus thought. But he didn't say it out loud. Everyone else looked so happy.

At that moment, Hera's feather flew back into her hand. She looked into the eye shape on the feather. Her smile faded quickly.

"Cronies!" she exclaimed. "About a dozen of them."

"Are they close?" Zeus asked worriedly.

The sound of thundering boots answered his question. And not only were the stamping boots loud, they made the earth shake. The Olympians were bounced around on it like they were on some kind of huge, weird trampoline!

"Let me guess," said Poseidon when he caught

his balance for a second. "We should run?" Suddenly, he was knocked off his feet again as the sound of boots got closer and closer.

"Run? Are you kidding? All I can do is bounce!" Zeus yelled. Every time he tried to move, another stomping *boom* made him topple over. The other Olympians were having a hard time staying upright too. If there hadn't been a bunch of Cronies on the way, it would almost be funny. But it wasn't. It was the opposite of funny!

As Zeus looked over at his friends bopping all over the place, he wondered what lay ahead for them all. What would the next battle bring for him? He hoped he could control his anger, be a good leader, and continue to make his mom proud. But he had to get back on his feet first!

Whoa! Those feet flew out from under him and he went flying. *Here we go again!* he thought as he crashed to the ground.